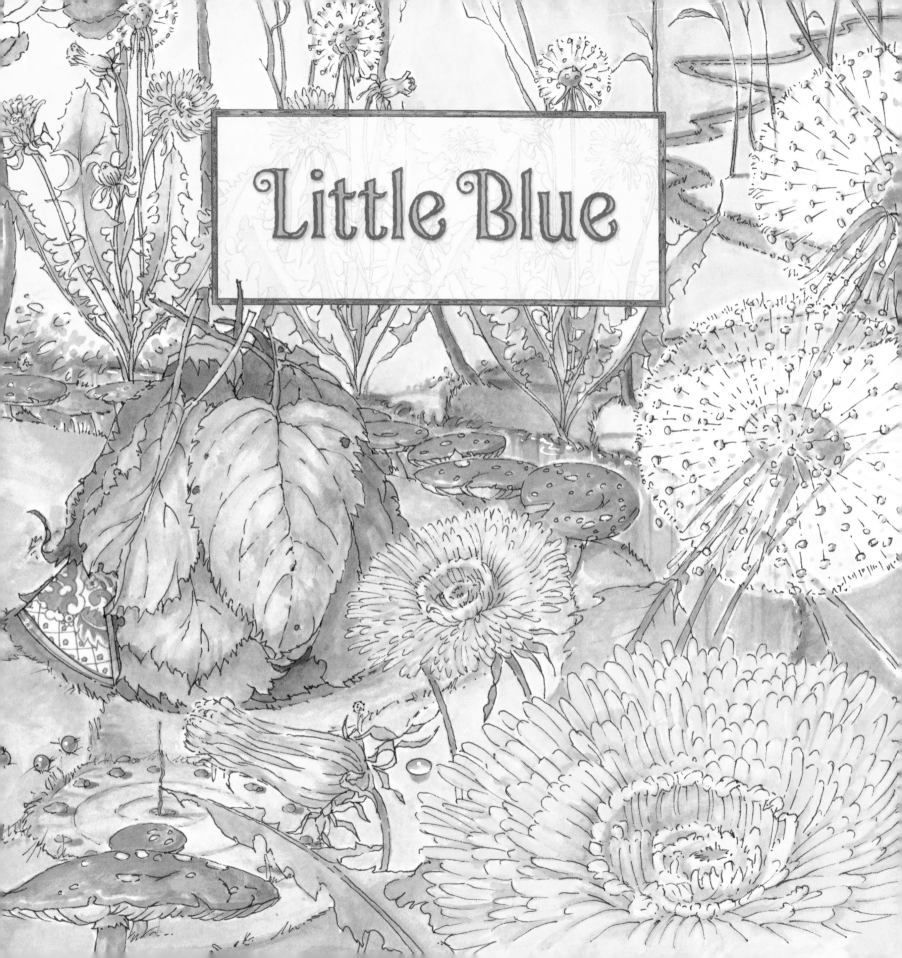

# Little Blue

*To Dick Weight, without whom there is no Home.*
*I am eternally indebted to Margrete Lamond and Jonathan Shaw.*
*Thank you to the May Gibbs Children's Literature Trust Artist*
*in Residence Program. ~ GCC*

Little Hare Books
8/21 Mary Street, Surry Hills
NSW 2010 AUSTRALIA
www.littleharebooks.com

National Library of Australia
Cataloguing-in-Publication entry

Chapman, Gaye Coralie.
Little Blue.

For children.
ISBN 978 1 921049 989 (hbk).

I. Title.

398.2094

Designed by Vida Kelly
Produced in Hong Kong by Bright Arts
Printed in China through Phoenix Offset

5 4 3 2 1  3968

Gaye Chapman

# Little Blue

LITTLE HARE
www.littleharebooks.com

Little Blue was lost.

She had waited long and called aloud.

She wanted to go home.

But no one came to find her.

Then, at long last, a boy came walking through the forest.
'Clink,' went his stick.

He had struck the shoe of a little blue girl.
'Who are you?' he asked.

'I am Little Blue. And I can't find my way home.'

'I am Will,' said the boy.

'What does your home look like?'

'My home has steps to the mountains,
and a wooden bridge.
I miss my mountains,' said Little Blue.

'My home has a path to the hills and the tall rocks.

Almost like your home,' said Will.

They climbed the hills and gazed from the rocks.

But they could not find the girl's way home.

'My home has a blue river
twinkling under willows.
I miss my river,' said Little Blue.

'My home has a stream bubbling over reeds.
Almost like your home,' said Will.
They rustled amongst the reeds and stared underwater.
But they could not find the girl's way home.

'My home has blue trees' said Little Blue,

'with apples like balls of sky. I really miss my apples.'

'My home has green trees, and blossoms like clouds.
Almost like your home,' said Will.
They climbed a tree and peered from the branches.
But they could not find the girl's way home.

'My home has a garden and a castle.
I really miss my castle,' said Little Blue.

'My home has an orchard and a cosy cottage.

Almost like your home,' said Will.

They picked the plums and looked under leaves.

But they could not find the girl's way home.

'My home has Father and bluebirds.
I really, really miss my father,' said Little Blue.

'My home has Grandmother and hens,' said Will.

'Almost like your home.'

They hunted under the hens and clambered over the gate.

'We have searched and searched,' said Little Blue.

'I will never find my way home.'

'You can come home with me,' said Will.

He held Little Blue in his hand and they went into the cottage together. 'Will!' cried Grandmother. 'You've found the little blue girl!'

And there on the dresser was a blue and white china plate.

There was a chip missing.

'She broke off,' said Grandmother, 'at a picnic long ago.'

Grandmother glued Little Blue back into the china plate.

'She's home,' said Will.

'Safe and sound,' said Grandmother, and made them both some tea.